When Stars Fell for Her

A Celestial Romance Beyond Time

by

Deepali

Lotus Sutra Books
www.lotussutrabooks.com

When Stars Fell for Her

This is a work of fiction. Names, characters, places, and incidents are products of the author's imagination or used fictitiously. Any resemblance to actual events, locales, or persons, living or dead, is purely coincidental.

Published by Lotus Sutra Books

www.lotussutrabooks.com

ISBN: 978-93-5592-276-2

Cover Design by WISE Studio

Edited by Lotus Sutra Books

First Edition, 2025

DEDICATION PAGE

—•✦•—

For those who believe love doesn't just find us — sometimes, it falls from the stars.

EPIGRAPH

–•✦•–

"And when the stars fell,

they whispered her name in the language of light."

ACKNOWLEDGMENTS

–•✦•–

This book would not exist without the stars that guided me — my family, my readers, and everyone who believed in Kritika's journey when she herself couldn't.

Thank you for letting me tell her story.

With love and starlight,

— *Deepali* ✨

PROLOGUE

–•✦•–

"When Stars Fell for Her" is the second installment in **The Star-bound Saga**, following *The Lies We Weave.*

You don't have to start with the first book — but you'll feel every heartbeat more deeply if you do.

TABLE OF CONTENTS

When Stars Fell for Her

By Deepali

Front Matter

- Title Page
- Copyright Page
- Dedication
- Acknowledgment
- Prologue — *The Last Echo*

Part I – The Fractured Balance

1. **The Last Echo**
   The ancient one's warning leaves the three allies shaken as the last realm collapses.
2. **Echoes of Fear**
   Trapped by their deepest fears, Kritika, Kael, and Aria confront the illusions of their past.
3. **The Fractured Realm**
   The trio begins their journey of self-discovery as illusions blur with reality.

4. **The Golden Gate**

   Reuniting with Master Vyas and Kritika's mother, they face the prophecy's awakening.

5. **The Shattered Sky**

   As chaos spreads, Master Vyas opens a new path and warns them to trust only balance.

Part II – The River of Memories

6. **Bay of Life**

   The trio meets Kritika's nani, guardian of the River of Life, where memories take form.

7. **The Ancient One Returns**

   A mysterious being emerges from the stars, testing their loyalty and faith.

8. **Shadows Between Stars**

   The allies uncover hidden truths about their origins and the worlds beyond.

9. **The Celestial Trial**

   Bound by prophecy, they face challenges set by a celestial council to prove their worth.

Part III – The Realm of Hearts

10. **Reflections of Truth**
    Each must face a mirror that reveals not who they are—but who they fear to become.
11. **Threads of Fate**
    Kael's past and Kritika's destiny intertwine as old bonds awaken forbidden emotions.
12. **The Rise of the Lost Star**
    Aria's power resurfaces, bridging the human realm and celestial gates once again.
13. **When Stars Fell for Her**
    As the worlds collide, Kritika must choose between love and the balance of all realms.

Back Matter

- Epilogue — *The Light Beyond Shadows*
- About the Author
- Series Teaser — *Book 3: The Whispering Realms*
- A Note to Readers

PROLOGUE

–•✦•–

Include a **brief recap paragraph** of *The Lies We Weave* for continuity:

Once, a lie began everything. Now, the truth will end it. Kritika's journey from illusion to balance has brought her across realms, through love, loss, and starlight. But when balance breaks again, and the stars themselves fall — destiny rewrites its name.

PROLOGUE – THE LIE THAT REACHED THE SKY

—•✦•—

When Kritika was small, she believed the stars were listening.

On hot monsoon nights in her grandmother's courtyard, she'd lie on the cool stone with her hair caught in the salt and jasmine of the air and whisper the silly, secret things that felt too large for a child's language. She whispered wishes into the dark, promises to future selves who smelled of old songbooks and 90s tapes, and she pretended she had a life that felt as steady as the constellations. Sometimes, in those hush-soft hours, a shooting star would cut across the sky and she would think the world had heard her.

The truth, later, would be less gentle: the world had listened, but it answered in a way she never expected.

Years after the courtyard's lanterns grew dim and after the lies had tumbled free like beads from a snapped string, Kritika had learned how consequences lived in small, ordinary things. A laugh that stopped mid-sentence. A group chat that no longer pinged. A face that looked through her instead of at her. She learned that to invent a love was to invent a debt the heart would demand back.

She had gone on, practical as a woman who mends torn hems and budgets for tiffin boxes: new college, new roommates, quieter corridors. She sang in rain-splashed toilets where sound swallowed shame. She drew constellations in the margins of her notebooks, careful, measured arcs and dots that, if nothing else, were honest.

And yet, at night, when the city's lights drowned the stars into a pale wash, she still dreamed.

On the night the mark came, she dreamed of a star that did not fall but folded itself like a living thing, a shard of light sliding down through the sky like a silver fish. It whispered a name in a voice made of distant radio static and forgotten lullabies. The name was hers — not the casual, public name, but the one her nani had used when she braided her hair: Kritika.

She woke with the taste of metal in her mouth and sunlight thinning across the wardrobe. When she reached to scratch the sleep from her wrist, her fingers paused. The skin bore a faint, raised map of pale burns — a constellation she had doodled as a child, the one she'd called *the Dreamer's Key*. Not the exact sketch she'd made in notebooks, but close enough to be the same idea, crystallized.

It shimmered when the morning light hit it, as if a tiny river ran beneath her skin. She pressed a thumb to the mark, felt a warmth that had nothing to do with fever, and for the first time since she had told the lie that had toppled her world, a small panic rose.

"Stars don't mark wrists," she told herself aloud, which is to say she tried to be sensible in a house where sense had been the first casualty of her adolescence. But as she prepared for college—the same one with the new buildings and a campus café that sold suspiciously good coffee—she could not shake the feeling that something old had been reached, some chord plucked in the sky by a tiny tremor she had caused long before she understood why.

When she left the building, sun pooling through the trees like light from a film set, she still wore her careful face: calm, organized. The city paid no heed to her constellated wrist. The street vendors called out for customers, scooters wove a metallic braid of sound. Life did what life does—it kept moving.

But the sky had changed.

For several nights after, the stars looked...too deliberate. Someone had rearranged them, a hand with a map. They blinked with patterns that could be mistaken for nothing more than astronomical curiosity. She would have called it superstition, except for how the nights began to hum softly, a frequency like distant traffic that made the hollow parts of her ribs vibrate. The hum matched the mark's warmth.

It was easier, for a girl who had learned the hard way that confession rarely returns exactly what you expect, to tuck the literal and figurative marks into the same drawer. But the drawer rattled, and the world kept catching on new threads of light.

That week, a storm rolled in from the sea—sheets of rain that made the city smell like iron. In the storm's sudden silver hush, as Kritika walked home with her backpack heavy with textbooks, a meteor flashed like a promise across the bruised sky. People looked up from their umbrellas and phones. A child screamed. A newscaster made a joke about falling stars. The meteor streaked and vanished as meteors do, but someone nearby pointed to the sky and said, more superstitiously than she'd intended, "A star fell. They say it means someone's fate is changing."

Kritika swallowed.

She had lied once about a boyfriend in a shirt that smelled like old cassettes and midnight streets—about a man who listened to her 90s songs and dedicated lines to her the way a lover would. She had told that lie as armor, as a way to shield herself from being the odd one out. The lie had grown bigger than its first lie-words. It had become a story that other people told in whispers, as if it were something separate from her. And she had watched, helpless, as the story took on a life of its own.

The mark pulsed beneath her sleeve, a slow heartbeat in the shape of a constellation. Somewhere above, the stars rearranged as if reading the margins of her life and writing back.

Sometimes the sky answers the question you did not know you asked.

CHAPTER ONE – THE ECHO OF LIES

—◦✦◦—

Kritika told herself the college would be a reset—plain coffee, new faces, a chance to be a ghost among people who'd never learned her name with the wrong weight behind it. The admissions office smelled like paper and disinfectant; the classrooms were newly painted, and the library windows threw the afternoon into wide, lazy rectangles.

It was, at first, ordinary in all the ways she needed: a corner seat at the art lab, sunlight catching dust motes as she sketched, headphones buffered against the world with a soundtrack of the 90s she had loved for as long as memory allowed. Drawing gave her control; lines didn't betray you when you lied. They simply became what you put them to be.

On a rain-dim morning a week later, when the university corridors were slick with student umbrellas and urgent footsteps, a new presence threaded across her periphery and broke the pattern of her days. He walked quietly, the kind of quiet that listened, not just for noise but for the rhythm beneath it. He had a jaw like a map of careful decisions, hair that fell in a way that made him look as if he'd stepped from a different photograph; his jacket had a faint, older smell—pine and something metallic, like the inside of an instrument case. People glanced. Or rather, people recognized: this new student carried the kind of silence that becomes a rumor in itself. He carried a stare that felt like an introduction.

She saw him standing by the notice board when class let out for lunch—lean, patient—studying flyers as if they were sacred texts. He was not immediately handsome in the obvious way; his face had angles that suggested thinking. But when he looked at her—when he turned, in a movement that seemed both casual and deliberate—something in the air clicked.

He recognized her. Or rather, he looked like someone who had always known where to find her in a crowd of faces.

She'd never met him. She opened her mouth to offer the usual polite smile one saves for strangers and found that the person who greeted her was not ordinary.

"Kritika Malhotra," he said. Not a question, not a guess. The name had a currency he did not use lightly.

Her fingers tightened around her sketchbook. "Do I know you?" she asked because one must ask, even of a sky-sent stranger, that small, civil question.

He tilted his head. There was no mocking in it, only an accuracy that made her uncomfortable. "You told a story once. It reached farther than you thought." His voice was low and threaded with a strange accent she couldn't place. "Because of that, I came."

She should have laughed then—dismissive, incredulous—but it came out like a cough. "Excuse me?" She tried to sound playful and landed somewhere between defensiveness and fear.

"You lied," he said simply, as if closing a book. "And lies, when shouted into emptiness, sometimes find an echo. I was listening."

The campus suddenly felt too small.

Kritika closed her sketchbook. "So you're... an echologist?" she asked, because the human thing to do in confusing situations is to make a joke.

He didn't smile. The barest crease touched the corner of his mouth—like someone trying on humor and deciding it didn't suit him. "You could call me a Fallen." He said the word like it was historical, not threatening. "A star that came down to see how the world was breathing."

That should have been impossible. Fallen stars did not stroll into campus cafeterias. Fallen stars lived in myths and were sold as trinkets on postcards.

"Nice to meet you, Star," she said, irreverence flattening her fear.

But he did not laugh. “I am not your star, Kritika.” The way he said her name made something in her chest quicken, as if the syllables themselves carried electricity. “You called me. Not in the loud, childish way. You called me with something you built to be true. I followed the fracture.”

Silence closed around them. People moved through the corridor, umbrellas and books and life, but the two of them were like a small island of stillness.

“What fracture?” she asked. Part of her wanted to step back—this was ridiculous. The other part, older and rawer, wanted to pull him closer and ask for the answer that had been missing for years. If a person could be an answer, that was what she’d needed.

He did not say what she expected: no sweeping cosmic explanation, no mention of gods. “The seam between what people *say* and what the world remembers,” he said. “Your stories have weight, Kritika. You build things with them. Sometimes the stars take notice.”

She tried to catalog: this was either a very elaborate prank or a mental breakdown waiting to be diagnosed. Both possibilities were equally unhelpful. “Why me?” she asked finally, voice small. “I said something stupid in school—”

"You said a lie," he interrupted, soft but unsparing. "It became a story. And stories, when repeated, become footprints across the sky."

The corners of her mouth twitched, involuntary. "So the sky is offended."

He looked at her for a long moment, eyes narrowing in a way that made her think of someone searching for a detail to latch onto. "Not offended. Curious. Also dangerous." He placed a hand on the wood of the notice board, as if to anchor himself in the normality of the room. "Because someone else can step through a story if you make it bright enough."

Her laugh was a sharp thing. "Who? Ghosts?"

He looked at her, and the strange gravity of his gaze made her think of nights in her nani's courtyard, of whispers in the dark. "People who are patient. People who wait for the smallest opening."

A retort rose to her lips—something about teenage melodrama, about how the world's cracks were usually a matter of cheap novels. She swallowed it. In the breadth of that corridor, words felt thin.

"Are you saying I—" she began.

He folded a paper from the board, a campus map, and slid it into his pocket almost as if the map mattered because it was a map, not because it contained secrets. "I'm saying that sometimes a truth has to be remembered by the sky for the sky to do anything. You made a truth beautiful. You leant it breath. Now the sky is breathing in your direction."

"What do you want?" The question came out harsher than she intended.

There was a flash in his eyes then—something that might have been pity or something that could have been interest, he wore it without embarrassment. "To know you," he said simply. "And to see whether you will choose what the world needs, or what you need."

For a moment she imagined being small and honest again, the way she had been as a child whispering into the night. She thought of the lie, and of how neatly it had fit into the spaces around her, the way it had swollen until it had no edges. She thought of friends on benches who trusted stories that were not theirs, of the sharp shame that followed.

She had always wanted someone to know her stories as if they were songs worth listening to. She had never planned for the listener to be made of sky.

The bell rang. Students poured into corridors and the island of stillness dissolved. He turned then, and for an odd second, she saw starlight in the hairs at his temple—their edges too precise, too out of place to belong.

"Call me Kael," he said over his shoulder, voice warming into something human. "If we are to be painfully literal—call me Kael."

She watched him move through the crowd and something like a small, risky hope folded in her chest. Maybe the world had rearranged itself in response to a careless lie. Maybe the universe liked stories. Maybe fallen stars liked company.

At the edge of the courtyard, he paused and looked back, and the brief silhouette of him against the sky cut the air like a question mark. His fingers brushed something invisible at his wrist. The small movement was private, intimate, almost ritual. He tucked his hands in his jacket and walked away.

When the day dimmed and the campus lights decided they could mimic constellations for the human eye, Kritika reached up to rub the little constellation on her wrist. It felt cooler now, as if it had settled like dust in a new place.

A lie, she thought—one that had been meant to protect—had grown teeth. And for the first time, the consequences had a face.

She drew in her notebook that night, lines pressed deep. The Dreamer's Key looked different under the lamplight: less like a childish sketch, more like a gateway. As she shaded the lines, she heard, distant and impossible, the faintest hum—like

radio static braided with a lullaby. The mark on her wrist warmed.
She closed the notebook and, for the first time in a long while, allowed herself to whisper to the sky the thing she had never told anyone: "If you're listening, don't be cruel."
The city gave no immediate answer. The hum, when it came, was a small thing like a pulse through a vein—patient and waiting. Somewhere, a star must have shifted.
Outside, in a different part of the night, the sky arranged a sentence of light no one else would understand: *She called. We came.*
And a boy named Kael, who had walked in silent halves across university corridors, had stepped where stories had made small cracks and bent down to look.

CHAPTER TWO — THE FRACTURE BENEATH THE SKY

–•✦•–

The first fracture wasn't in the sky.

It was in the way the air bent around Kael.

That morning, the city looked washed clean after a night of storm—pavements glazed with leftover rain, and the smell of wet cement rising like a promise of renewal. Kritika reached college early, half on purpose, half because sleep had refused her. Her mind kept looping over the stranger's words.

You called me.

She sat on the last bench of the art studio, pretending to lose herself in charcoal dust and unfinished sketches. Outside, the jacaranda trees leaned close to the window, whispering things leaves shouldn't know. The world felt just slightly... off. The clock's ticking was too loud. Her reflection in the window blinked a half-second slower than she did.

She looked down at her wrist. The constellation glimmered faintly, almost shy, like it was breathing beneath her skin.

"Beautiful," a voice said.

Kritika's pencil rolled off the table. Kael stood by the door — quiet, composed, the same soft disarray in his hair. He hadn't changed clothes, she noticed. Or maybe they were just always this clean, this unwrinkled, as if he didn't belong to time the way humans did.

"You followed me?" she asked.

"I followed the sound." He stepped closer, eyes glancing at the mark on her wrist. "It hums. Do you feel it?"

"No," she said quickly, pulling her sleeve down. "And stop saying weird things. You sound like a podcast about aliens."

Kael smiled — barely. "Then maybe you should listen harder."

The air between them thickened — a silence that hummed. And then, from somewhere behind them, a mirror cracked.

It was a clean sound — like a line drawn across glass. Kritika flinched. When she turned, she saw her reflection divided neatly down the middle, one half slightly *late* in motion.

"Coincidence," she whispered.

Kael crouched, picked up a piece of the fallen glass. The shard reflected him twice — one clear, one blurred. "Coincidences are just unpracticed patterns," he murmured, and dropped it gently onto the table.

"Why are you here?" Kritika asked again, voice steadier now.

Kael looked out the window. "The stars don't fall without reason. When a truth breaks, we come to mend it."

"Mend?"

He nodded once. "There's a Fracture forming — between

what's remembered and what's real. You built the story. You'll have to close it."

Kritika laughed, sharp and tired. "I'm a 22-year-old student who failed her psychology elective. I'm not a cosmic engineer."

"Maybe not." His eyes softened. "But you're a storyteller. You created something powerful enough that it woke us."

The word *us* hung in the air like a warning.

Before she could respond, the classroom door opened, and a familiar voice cut through the haze.

"Are you still sketching your conspiracies?"

Kritika turned — and froze.

It was **Moni.**

Her oldest friend. The one she'd lied *for*. The one who'd stopped answering her messages after graduation. But Moni wasn't supposed to be here. She studied in a different city.

"Hey..." Kritika's throat tightened. "How—"

Moni smiled, too easily. "Long story. Thought I'd visit." She walked inside, her footsteps unnaturally soft, almost floating. Her hand trailed over the broken glass, leaving no cuts.

Kritika's heart stuttered. The mark on her wrist *burned.*

Kael's tone changed, low and clipped. "Step back, Kritika."

"What—"

"That's not her."

Moni's smile twitched. For a moment, the air rippled behind her, like heat waves bending light. The outline of her face flickered — an echo, not a person.

"You wanted to fix what you broke," the *echo* said, her voice layered with static. "But some truths are meant to haunt you."

Then she vanished — dissolved into thin motes of light that shimmered, then disappeared.

Kritika stood shaking. "What the hell was that?"

Kael exhaled. "The first echo. A memory the world tried to keep alive."

"Are you saying she's—"

He shook his head. "She exists. But so does her shadow. The Fracture feeds on your memories, Kritika. Every regret, every unfinished sentence—it makes them *real*."

She pressed her hands to her ears, trying to ground herself. "No. No. I'm done with all this—stars, lies, ghosts."

Kael stepped closer, gently placing a hand on her wrist. His touch was cool, like moonlight. "Then listen to me," he said softly. "You can end it. But you'll have to walk through it first."

Something in his voice—honest, ancient—cut through her panic. She looked up, eyes catching his. For a second, she saw the night sky reflected in them — galaxies folded small enough to fit inside human irises.

And in that moment, she realized the impossible truth: The boy standing in front of her wasn't human.

He wasn't a fantasy or a ghost. He was a *response.*

The stars had fallen, and one of them had chosen her.

CHAPTER THREE – THE STAR-BORN AND THE LIAR

—◦✦◦—

The silence that followed wasn't empty. It throbbed – like something vast and unseen was breathing just outside the walls.

Kritika could still feel Kael's hand on her wrist, faint warmth fading into her pulse. The broken mirror behind them had turned dull, the shimmer gone, but the memory of Moni's echo lingered – her voice, her half-smile, that wrongness that felt too real.

Her heart was hammering. "You said she exists," she whispered. "Then where is she? What did I just see?"

Kael didn't look at her. His eyes were on the window, on the violet haze crawling across the morning sky. "You saw what the Fracture wants you to remember," he said quietly. "You lied once – not out of cruelty, but fear. That lie tore something open. Now everything you've buried is trying to crawl back through."

Kritika pressed her palms to her temples. "I didn't– I didn't mean to cause any of this."

"No one ever does," Kael said, voice almost kind. "But meaning doesn't undo impact. That's what makes truth dangerous."

She gave him a sharp look. "You talk like you've done this before."

He hesitated. The air shimmered faintly around him — like a mirage made of light. "I have," he admitted. "I've watched countless worlds fracture because of a single unspoken truth. But this—" He looked at her wrist, then at her. "This is different."

"How?"

Kael stepped closer. "Because this time, the liar didn't just make the story—she believed it."

The words hit her like a physical shove. The room tilted, just slightly.

Images flickered through her mind — the school courtyard, whispered rumours, Moni's terrified eyes the night of the confrontation, the flash of light before everything changed.

She'd told everyone she didn't know what happened. She'd told herself that too.

"Stop," she whispered, clutching her head. "Stop showing me—"

"I'm not," Kael said. "You are."

Her mark pulsed — harder this time, like it was alive. A thin thread of light wound up her arm, fracturing into faint symbols across her skin. The temperature dropped. The ceiling light flickered, sputtered, then went out.

Kael's voice lowered. "You're awakening it faster than I expected."

"What *it*?"

"The mark. The bond. The reason I'm here."

He lifted his hand, showing his palm. Faint constellations shimmered across it — the same pattern as hers, reversed, glowing like two sides of a mirror.

Kritika stepped back instinctively. "What are you doing?"

"I'm showing you the truth."

"Don't," she said sharply. "I've had enough of truths."

"You haven't even started."

Kael closed his fingers into a fist, and the air between them bent — as though space itself inhaled. The shards of the broken mirror lifted, swirling slowly, reflecting light like silver snow.

"You called for help," he said. "Your soul wanted balance, not absolution. I was sent because the stars heard you before you did."

Kritika stared, her throat tight. "You're insane."

Kael gave a faint, rueful smile. "Possibly. But so are you."

The lights flickered back to life with a faint hum. Everything looked normal again — too normal. The glass lay still, Kael's glow gone, and the world resumed pretending it hadn't just bent around them.

Kritika sat down slowly, her knees weak. "If this is real," she said carefully, "then there must be rules. What are they?"

Kael's expression darkened. "Every lie you told created a reflection — a version of you that believed the opposite. The Fracture feeds on those reflections. The only way to seal it... is to face them."

"Face *myself?*"

"Every version of yourself," he corrected. "And not all of them want to die."

She swallowed, staring at her trembling hands. "You make it sound like some fantasy punishment."

Kael tilted his head. "You wrote fantasies once, didn't you?"

Kritika blinked. "What?"

He nodded toward her bag. "The notebook. You wrote stories where the world could bend to emotion. Where lies could shape destinies."

Her pulse quickened. The notebook — the one she'd written during the worst year of her life. She hadn't opened it in months.

"How do you know that?" she asked quietly.

Kael looked at her, and for the first time, something human flickered in his expression — guilt. “Because your words reached farther than you thought. They built echoes. Worlds. Me.”

The room spun again, slower this time, like reality was being peeled layer by layer.

Kritika exhaled, her voice cracking. “Then tell me, Kael. What happens when lies become worlds?”

He met her eyes — calm, almost sad. “They fall,” he said softly. “And someone has to catch them before they shatter everything else.”

CHAPTER FOUR – ECHOES OF WHAT WAS LOST

–•✦•–

That night, Kritika dreamt in static.

Every sound was slightly distorted—like an old cassette tape playing a memory she didn't want to hear again. The rain outside her apartment fell in a rhythm too even, too precise. The clock on the wall ticked backward. And when she opened her eyes, her ceiling wasn't there.

Instead, there was sky.

A violet-black expanse stretched above her, dotted with silver constellations forming and reforming faster than thought. She was floating—not falling, not flying—just *suspended* in the kind of silence that felt older than creation.

"You're dreaming," said a voice behind her.

Kritika turned. Kael stood in the void, his presence pulling light toward him. He looked exactly as before, except his eyes—his eyes were no longer human. They reflected galaxies. She tried to speak, but her words came out in echoes. "Why... am I here?"

"This isn't a place," Kael said. "It's a fracture. A memory disguised as a dream."

Kritika frowned. "Whose memory?"

Kael's gaze softened. "Yours."

The stars dimmed. And suddenly, she was standing on a wet school courtyard—her old school. The same one where everything began. The sky turned the color of bruised twilight. She saw herself, younger, laughing with Moni under the banyan tree. The sound was faint, like hearing joy through water.

Kritika's throat tightened. "No. Not this."

Kael's voice was low. "You need to see it."

The memory shifted—the laughter vanished. The echo of her younger self stood frozen, eyes wide. Across the yard, figures in cloaks appeared—the secret society members. Their voices were indistinguishable murmurs. One of them stepped forward, removing her hood.

Kritika's breath caught. Her mother.

The woman's eyes, calm and sharp, met her daughter's even across the boundary of memory. "You're not ready," she said—not to the child, but to *her*. The present Kritika. "But you must remember what you chose."

The air cracked open like lightning. The younger Kritika screamed, a flare of white light bursting from her hands, throwing the shadows back.

Kritika fell to her knees. "I didn't mean—"

Kael's hand rested gently on her shoulder. "I know. But meaning doesn't erase what happened."

The scene flickered. Moni's echo appeared again, this time not cruel—just broken. "You said you'd never lie to me," the echo whispered.

"I didn't—"

"You did," Moni said. "You lied to protect me. But the truth doesn't need protection. It needs courage."

Kritika reached for her, but the echo dissolved into raindrops that hung suspended in the air, each drop reflecting a different version of her face.

She whispered, "I can't do this."

Kael's voice was steady. "You already are."

The stars reappeared above them, brighter now. One descended—a single falling star—landing softly beside them, pulsing like a heartbeat. Kael picked it up and pressed it into her palm.

"This," he said quietly, "is what remains of what you lost. Your truth doesn't destroy—it transforms. But you have to stop running from it."

The warmth spread through her hand, up her arm, into her chest. The mark on her wrist glowed brighter, forming a small ring of light. She looked up at Kael. "You talk like you've done this before."

Kael smiled faintly. “I told you. I mend what breaks.”

“And what about you? Who mends you?”

He looked away, his expression unreadable. “No one.”

Something in his voice ached—something she recognized too well. The sound of someone who’s spent lifetimes fixing everyone else’s damage while letting his own bleed quietly.

Kritika exhaled, the tears she hadn’t realized were forming finally falling. “You’re not as untouchable as you pretend to be, are you?”

Kael’s eyes met hers. “Neither are you.”

The space between them shimmered, and suddenly they were back in her room—the clock ticking correctly, the window reflecting only one version of her face.

For the first time in a long time, the silence felt... real.

Kritika looked down at the fading light on her wrist, then back at Kael. “What now?”

He stood at the window, his silhouette framed by the city lights. “Now, we prepare. The echoes are just the beginning.”

She frowned. “Beginning of what?”

He turned to her, eyes glowing faintly with starlight.

“The return of the fallen star.”

CHAPTER FIVE – THE RETURN OF THE FALLEN STAR

—◦✦◦—

The world didn't return to normal after the dream.

Kritika woke with the taste of starlight in her mouth – metallic, electric, unreal. Her heartbeat carried a rhythm she didn't recognize, like a melody humming beneath her skin. The faint ring of light on her wrist pulsed with every beat, and each pulse whispered a word she couldn't quite hear.

Outside, Delhi was just waking up. The city was grey and wet, horns echoing through streets half-buried in smog. To anyone else, it was an ordinary morning. But Kritika knew better – something had shifted.

And Kael was gone.

She called out, half expecting him to step out of the shadows like he always did – calm, cryptic, infuriatingly composed. But the room was empty, and the air felt heavier, as if reality itself hadn't fully settled after the dream.

Then her phone buzzed.

Unknown Number: *"Meet me where it all began."*

Her throat tightened. The words weren't signed, but she didn't need them to be. She already knew.

The school.

The one she'd left behind, the one that still lived in the corners of her nightmares.

The old gates of St. Helena's School were rusted now, streaked with the weight of forgotten years. Kritika stood there, umbrella in hand, staring at the peeling blue paint that once framed her laughter. The banyan tree was still there — twisted, enormous, and older than memory itself.

The wind shifted. Someone was waiting by the tree.

He wore the same dark coat, but something about him had changed. The mark on Kael's wrist glowed faintly, the same pattern that now shimmered beneath her skin.

"You came," he said quietly.

"I had to," she replied, her voice tight. "You left without saying anything."

Kael's gaze softened. "If I'd stayed, you would've tried to stop me. And I can't afford that."

"What are you talking about?"

He looked past her, to the empty classrooms, to the sky turning a strange shade of violet again. "The fracture you saw — it wasn't just a dream. The echoes are spreading. And it's my fault."

Kritika's brows furrowed. "Your fault?"

Kael nodded. “You think I found you by accident? I didn’t. I was sent here... because I fell.”

Her stomach twisted. “Fell?”

He looked up — the light in his eyes dimming to something human, something almost fragile. “I’m not supposed to be here. I’m one of the Starbound — celestial sentinels meant to guard the balance between realms. But I broke the order. I crossed into your world for something forbidden.”

Kritika’s voice dropped. “What?”

He hesitated, his voice barely above a whisper. “You.”

The rain froze midair.

For a moment, she couldn’t breathe. Her heart pounded against her ribs, the ring of light on her wrist flaring bright enough to illuminate both of them.

“Don’t,” she said weakly. “Don’t say things you don’t mean.”

“I don’t say things I don’t mean,” he replied, stepping closer. “When I first saw you, I thought you were a fracture — a mistake in the weave of fate. But then I realized something worse. You were the reason the stars began to fall.”

Her hands trembled. “What are you saying?”

“That your world isn’t breaking because of the lies you told,” Kael said softly. “It’s breaking because of what you are.”

Kritika staggered back, shaking her head. “I’m not—”

"You are," he interrupted. "You're the mortal vessel for what was once known as the 'Heart of Aether.' The bridge between realities. Every realm is tied to you — your emotions, your choices, your truths. When you lie, worlds fracture. When you break, dimensions crumble."

Her voice cracked. "And when I love?"

Kael's eyes locked with hers. "Then stars fall."

Lightning split the sky, thunder echoing across the courtyard. The banyan tree shuddered as roots burst from the ground, glowing veins of blue-white energy crawling across the earth.

Kael reached for her hand. "They've found us."

"Who?"

"The ones who want the Heart. They've been waiting since the first lie was spoken."

And then she saw them — shadows forming at the edge of the playground, eyes like molten gold. They didn't move like humans; they rippled, each step dissolving and reforming their bodies like smoke caught in wind.

Kael pulled her close. "Remember what I said — don't run from the truth."

And before she could respond, the world shattered into starlight.

CHAPTER SIX – THE HEART OF AETHER

—◦✦◦—

The world didn't break this time.

It folded.

One blink, and Kritika was no longer standing in the courtyard. The ground beneath her shimmered like glass, reflecting a thousand versions of herself – some smiling, some crying, some... gone. The sky above was not a sky at all but a swirling vortex of stars trapped in slow motion, each one pulsing in rhythm with her heartbeat.

Kael was beside her, his coat flickering between light and shadow. The air was thin, trembling with a low hum that felt almost alive.

"Where are we?" Kritika whispered, her voice small in the infinite expanse.

Kael's gaze swept the horizon. "Between worlds. The In-Between Realm. The place where truth and illusion meet before becoming reality."

She looked down at the glass beneath her feet, watching one reflection dissolve into smoke. "Why bring me here?"

"Because this," Kael said, his voice quieter now, "is where the Heart of Aether was first born. And where it died."

The words hung heavy, ancient. A gust of wind stirred the air, carrying with it faint echoes — laughter, screams, the clash of energy long faded. Kritika wrapped her arms around herself.

"You said I was its vessel. What does that mean?"

Kael didn't answer right away. Instead, he crouched and brushed his hand against the ground. A ripple spread outward, revealing a vision — an image woven from light.

A temple made of crystal. A figure standing at its center, cloaked in silver flame. Her face was hidden, but her posture was unmistakable — graceful, fierce, fragile all at once.

"That's her," Kael said. "The original Heart. The Star who loved a mortal."

Kritika's pulse quickened. "A Star... fell in love?"

"Yes," Kael replied, his tone edged with something mournful. "And because of that love, the balance was broken. The realms began to collapse, one by one. When she died, her essence scattered through the skies — fragments of her soul became the stars you see now. And one fragment... found its way into a human child."

Kritika felt her breath catch.

"You're saying—"

He nodded. "That fragment is you."

Her knees felt weak. "No. That's not possible. I'm just—"

"Just a girl?" Kael's eyes softened. "That's exactly what she was, too."

For a long moment, there was silence — the kind that carries weight, meaning, inevitability.

Then, the glass beneath them trembled. A fissure of light ran through the ground, splitting one of the reflections in half. Kael immediately stepped in front of her, his hand glowing with faint starlight.

"They're trying to break through," he said under his breath.

"Who?"

"The Collectors," he said. "They can smell the Heart's energy now. They want to use it to reopen the fallen gate."

The fissure widened. Shadows crawled through it, whispering in voices too soft to be human. Kritika staggered back, her hand brushing against one of the floating shards of light — and suddenly, she was somewhere else.

She stood in a classroom — *her* classroom — empty except for Moni sitting on a desk, legs swinging, a familiar mischievous smile on her lips.

"Moni?"

Her old friend tilted her head. "You still don't get it, do you?"

Kritika blinked. "Get what?"

"That the past doesn't stay buried. You can't run from what made you who you are."

Kritika reached for her, but Moni's image began to dissolve, leaving behind only the echo of her laughter — and a whisper.

"Forgive yourself before it's too late."

She gasped, pulling back into the In-Between Realm. Kael was gripping her arm, his expression strained. "Don't touch the shards! They feed on memory."

"I saw her," Kritika said shakily. "Moni. She—"

Kael's jaw tightened. "The shards show what still binds you. The Heart won't awaken until you've let go."

"I can't just forget her!"

"I didn't say forget," Kael replied. "I said forgive."

The wind howled, and the cracks beneath them began to glow violently. Kael reached out his hand. "You have to trust me."

Kritika hesitated. "Last time I trusted someone, it broke everything."

His gaze held hers — steady, burning. "Then maybe this time, it'll fix something."

She took his hand.

Instantly, the shards around them lifted, spiraling into the air, forming a luminous sphere. It pulsed once — twice — then burst, showering them with light. The force knocked them both backward, but when the glow faded, the ground beneath them had changed.

They were standing on solid stone now — inside the very temple from Kael's vision.

At the altar, a single object floated — a crystalline heart, beating slowly, wrapped in threads of silver and gold. The **Heart of Aether.**

Kritika stepped forward, the light from her wrist resonating with it. Every step made the temple hum louder, as if it recognized her.

Kael whispered, "It's responding to you."

She turned toward him. "What happens if I touch it?"

He hesitated. "You'll remember everything. Every life, every lie, every truth tied to your soul. But it will also change you."

Her hand hovered over the heart, trembling. "And if I don't?"

"Then the realms fall," Kael said simply.

She looked up, her eyes glistening. "I'm scared."

"So am I," he whispered. "But maybe we were both meant to fall — just not apart."

She closed her eyes… and touched the Heart.

Light exploded.

Memories flooded in — flashes of countless lives, faces she'd never seen, and one voice echoing through all of them: *"When stars fall, they fall for love."*

CHAPTER SEVEN — THE FALLEN REMEMBER

–•✦•–

The world spun — but not like before.

This time, it wasn't pain that tore through her. It was recognition.

Kritika blinked, and suddenly, the temple melted away. The Heart of Aether was no longer in front of her — it was inside her, pulsing faintly like a second heartbeat. Every thrum of it opened a window, and through each one, fragments of another world poured into her mind.

The sky was made of gold fire. Rivers ran with silver light. Mountains glowed from within, carved from crystal. And at the center of it all stood a city that breathed — **Elarion**, the Celestial Citadel.

She gasped as the visions deepened. The people weren't human; their forms shimmered, translucent, carved from starfire and thought. Each being carried a mark on their chest — a constellation etched in light.

Among them, one glowed brighter than the rest. A woman.

Her face was familiar, painfully so. Kritika reached out — and the woman moved in perfect synchrony. It was her. Or rather, what she once was.

"Lira," whispered a voice.

Kritika turned. Kael stood there — not as she knew him now, but radiant, his form cloaked in celestial armor, eyes alive with energy. But his aura was... warmer. Unburdened.

She suddenly understood: this wasn't just a vision. This was memory.

And *Kael had been there, too.*

Lira — the first fallen star — stood before the Council of Aetherians.

The grand hall blazed with constellations that shimmered like living maps of creation. A being with a crown of comets spoke:

"You have defied the order, Lira of the Eastern Veil. You crossed into mortal skies. You broke the divide."

Her voice was steady, though her hands trembled.

"I crossed because I saw something you refused to see — love does not divide. It unites."

Whispers rippled through the chamber like storm winds.

Another voice, colder:

"Love is imperfection. It taints the eternal with mortality. The Heart cannot exist in both worlds."

Lira lifted her chin.

"Then let it burn. I would rather feel for one lifetime than live in eternity numb."

Kritika's heart pounded — she knew these words before she even heard them.

She remembered *saying* them.

The council's light flared, blinding.

"Then you will fall."

And so she did.

She fell from the heavens, tearing through clouds and chaos, her wings of starlight crumbling into dust. The sky screamed as she descended — and when she opened her eyes again, she was lying beside a river under a mortal sky.

And there he was. young man, drenched from the rain, eyes wide, reaching out to her as if afraid she might vanish.

Kael.

Not celestial. Not eternal. Just human. He whispered, "You fell."

And she, still dazed, smiled faintly. "Then catch me."

The visions fractured like glass struck by a hammer. Kritika gasped, collapsing to her knees. Her heart burned — the same ache, the same longing that didn't belong to this life but felt like it had always been there.

Kael knelt beside her, his expression unreadable. "You remember now," he said softly.

Her voice shook. "That was us... wasn't it?"

He didn't answer. The silence said enough.

She stared at him, anger and sorrow twisting together. "All this time — you knew. You knew who I was."

"I couldn't tell you," Kael replied, his tone heavy with restraint. "The laws of the Starbound forbid interference with mortal lives. I broke that once for you — and it shattered everything. If I did it again, there'd be no turning back."

Tears welled in her eyes. "You let me think I was going insane. You let me believe I was just... broken."

He stepped closer, his hand hovering near her face but not touching. "You weren't broken, Kritika. You were waking up."

The temple trembled. The Heart within her pulsed faster, its light spilling out through her veins. She clutched her chest, gasping. "It hurts."

Kael's jaw tightened. "Because it's remembering everything it lost. The first Heart was never meant to feel twice — and now it's alive again."

The air cracked, and a voice echoed through the realm — deep, echoing, almost divine.

"The fallen remember. The fracture grows."

Kael stiffened. "They found us."

Before Kritika could ask who, shadows flooded the temple floor — thousands of golden eyes glinting in the dark. The Collectors.

Kael grabbed her hand. “We can’t fight them here.”

“Where are we going?”

He looked toward the far wall, where the stars began to rearrange themselves into a door of pure light. “To where it all began — before the fall.”

The Heart of Aether pulsed once more, its glow wrapping around them like a cocoon. Kritika’s last thought before everything vanished was not fear, but realization —

That maybe, the reason stars fell wasn’t because of love. It was because love was the only thing worth falling for.

CHAPTER EIGHT — THE CELESTIAL MARK

– • ✦ • –

When Kritika opened her eyes, she was standing in a place that did not belong to time.

The world around her glowed in shades of deep indigo and soft gold, like dusk trapped in an eternal loop. The ground beneath her feet shimmered faintly, reflecting constellations that moved — alive, whispering in forgotten languages.

Kael stood a few steps away, his back turned, his shoulders rigid. The silence between them was heavier than the realm itself.

Kritika took a hesitant step forward. “Where are we?”

Kael didn’t look at her. “The Archive of Stars. The first sky ever formed. Every truth ever spoken or buried is written here.”

She glanced up. The heavens above were covered in intricate lines of light, crisscrossing to form endless patterns — stories, prophecies, names. One line pulsed faintly, like a heartbeat.

Her name.

She reached out. The moment her fingertips brushed it, a sharp pain pierced her chest — an image flooding her mind.

Kael, bound in chains of light, kneeling before the same Council that had cursed her.

"Kael..." she whispered.

The vision deepened.

He was shouting, voice echoing across the chamber.

"It was my fault! I called her down. I begged her to fall!"

The Celestial Council watched in silence. Their leader, the one crowned in comets, finally spoke:

"Then you, too, shall bear the mark of the fallen. You will live and die across lifetimes — always remembering her, never saving her."

Kael's body arched in agony as a symbol seared across his skin — a spiral of starlight and shadow that wrapped around his wrist.

The same one she had seen glowing on his arm.

The vision shattered. Kritika stumbled back, tears stinging her eyes.

"You lied to me," she whispered. "You said you came here because you fell. But you didn't fall... You were *banished*."

Kael turned slowly, his expression haunted. "Does it matter?"

"Yes!" Her voice broke. "Because it means everything you've done — saving me, helping me — wasn't out of choice. It was punishment."

He flinched. “You think I would endure centuries of this just because I was ordered to? Kritika, I—”

“Don’t!” she snapped. “Don’t call me that like it means something. You’ve known who I was all along, haven’t you? You knew the Heart was inside me. That’s why you came back.”

Kael stepped closer, his voice trembling despite the calm he tried to hold. “I came because I couldn’t not. Every time I tried to forget, your name burned inside my mind. Every time I looked at the stars, they whispered your face. You think that’s duty?”

Kritika’s eyes glistened. “Then what is it?”

“Curse,” he said softly. “And love. Both.”

The air shimmered — constellations above them began to move, rearranging into shapes that burned brighter than before. Kritika’s mark flared again, resonating with his. The space between them rippled, as if reality itself was holding its breath.

She whispered, “You should’ve told me.”

“And if I did?” Kael’s voice cracked. “Would you have believed me? Or hated me sooner?”

Her lips parted, but she had no answer.

Then, as if sensing the truth finally exposed, the realm darkened. The stars began to dim, their light flickering like dying candles.

Kael looked up sharply. “They know.”

“Who?”

“The Council,” he said grimly. “They felt the Heart awaken. They’ll try to erase us — both of us. Again.”

He turned to her, eyes fierce. “If they come, promise me you’ll run.”

“I’m done running,” Kritika said firmly. “All my life, I’ve been hiding — from the truth, from my lies, from myself. Not anymore.”

The words carried power — her mark glowed so brightly that the air itself trembled. The ground cracked open, and a pillar of light shot upward, cutting through the dark sky like a sword.

Kael grabbed her arm. “Kritika! You’re drawing too much energy—”

She looked at him, tears and determination blending in her gaze. “Then maybe it’s time they remember what a fallen star can do.”

The pillar erupted, blinding the realm in white fire.

When the light faded, only silence remained.

And somewhere above them, the constellations shifted — a new one forming in the heavens. Two intertwined spirals of light.

The mark of the fallen and the heart reborn.

CHAPTER NINE — THE CONSTELLATION WAR

– • ✦ • –

The light faded slowly, leaving the air dense with the scent of smoke and stardust.

Kritika stood at the center of a shattered world — the Archive of Stars was collapsing around her. The constellations above cracked like glass, fragments of celestial fire raining down into the void. The ground pulsed beneath her feet, veins of molten gold racing outward like lightning frozen in motion.

Kael was on one knee, gripping his chest where his mark still glowed fiercely. “They’re coming,” he said hoarsely. “The Council knows we’ve broken the laws.”

Kritika turned to him, the faint ring on her wrist burning brighter. “Then let them come.”

A distant hum filled the air — harmonic at first, then rising to a deafening roar. The sky split open, and through it descended the armies of light. Celestial Sentinels — beings of pure energy, wings forged from constellations, eyes like suns. They were magnificent and terrifying, each one carrying the symbol of the Council across their armor.

At their head, the **Archon of the Celestial Order** descended, his voice echoing like thunder wrapped in melody.

"Lira of the Fallen Light. Kael of the Banished Flame. You stand accused of defiance against creation itself."

Kritika clenched her fists. "I am not Lira. I am Kritika. And I'm not defying creation — I'm trying to save it!"

The Archon's golden eyes glimmered.

"Creation does not need saving. It needs obedience."

Kael stepped beside her, his aura flaring silver. "Then you'll have to destroy us both."

"So be it."

The heavens erupted.

The first wave hit with the force of a collapsing sun. Kael raised his hand, summoning a shield of starfire that barely held. The impact sent ripples through the void, fracturing the glass-like ground. Kritika's heart raced; she felt the Heart of Aether surge inside her, begging to be released.

She reached out, instinct guiding her — and the world responded. Stars bent, realigned, and formed a barrier around them. Light curved in impossible shapes, her thoughts turning into weapons of pure will.

Kael looked at her, awe flickering through the chaos. “You’re doing it.”

“I’m not doing anything,” she breathed. “It’s... alive.”

The Heart pulsed in rhythm with her heartbeat, amplifying every emotion. Fear became shields. Love became energy. Rage became power.

But power came with pain. Every burst of light tore through her veins like fire. The mark on her wrist spread up her arm, tracing its way toward her heart.

“Kritika, stop!” Kael shouted. “You’re burning yourself out!”

She screamed through the pain, eyes blazing with defiance. “I can’t stop! If I do, they’ll kill us both!”

He darted forward, catching her wrist, their marks colliding — and suddenly, the world froze.

Every Sentinel halted mid-flight. The air crystallized.

A blinding flash erupted where their hands met, and a massive surge of energy shot outward, knocking the Celestial armies back into the stars.

When the light dimmed, silence reigned once again.

Kritika collapsed, trembling. “What... just happened?”

Kael stared at their wrists. The two marks had fused — forming a new sigil neither of them had seen before: a spiral of gold and silver intertwined, the *Celestial Mark of Unity*.

"The Heart and the Banished Flame," Kael whispered. "They've never joined before."

Before he could say more, the Archon rose again from the debris, his armor cracked, his glow flickering.

"You have no idea what you've done," he hissed. "You've undone the boundaries between realms. The Heart cannot coexist with the Fallen Flame. The balance will collapse."

Kritika's voice was weak but steady. "Maybe it's time balance stopped being built on sacrifice."

The Archon's eyes narrowed. "Then let the universe burn with your love."

He raised his staff — and the stars screamed.

The sky tore open, revealing a massive rift in the fabric of creation. The Collectors emerged again, drawn by the chaos — their golden eyes hungry, their forms writhing. The Sentinels turned on them instantly, chaos exploding across every plane of existence.

Kael grabbed Kritika, pulling her into the shadow of a falling fragment of sky. "We need to close the rift!"

"How?" she shouted over the noise.

"You have the Heart — I have the Flame. Together, we can seal it. But..."

"But what?"

He hesitated. "It'll cost us everything."

Kritika met his gaze — terrified, furious, and still in love. "Then we'll give it everything."

They joined hands, pressing their palms together. The sigil between them flared, and the world bent inward. The Heart's light and the Flame's fire collided, forming a vortex of raw energy.

The rift began to close — stars screaming as they were pulled back into alignment. The Sentinels retreated, the Collectors scattered into ash.

As the last echo of the rift sealed, Kritika felt the weight of eternity crush her chest.

She saw Kael's eyes — soft, sad, proud.

"Don't let go," she whispered.

"I never did," he said.

And then, everything went white.

CHAPTER TEN – THE PRICE OF TRUTH

–•✦•–

When the light faded, there was nothing.

No sound. No color. No heartbeat. Just stillness – the kind that feels like it's waiting to see who survived.

Kritika opened her eyes to a world washed in grey. The air shimmered faintly, bending in and out of focus like an unfinished dream. Her fingers twitched against cool, cracked glass – the same kind that had once made up the floor of the In-Between Realm. But now, it was fractured beyond recognition.

She sat up slowly, her breath trembling. Her mark had dimmed. The silver and gold swirl on her wrist pulsed faintly, like a dying ember.

"Kael?"

No answer.

Her voice broke a little. "Kael!"

Her echo came back – small, fragile, unreturned.

The silence that followed was unbearable.

Kritika stumbled to her feet, eyes scanning the ruins of the realm. The stars above were broken – jagged shards of light frozen mid-fall. In the distance, the remnants of constellations floated like ghostly outlines in the dark.

She pressed her hand to her chest. The Heart of Aether was still inside her, but its rhythm was slower now — quieter. Like it, too, was grieving.

"Where are you?" she whispered.

For the first time, the universe didn't answer.

She walked.

Through fields of broken light. Through echoes of her own memories — laughter, screams, a single falling star. Time had no meaning here; every step could've been a second or a century.

Her thoughts came in fragments.

He said don't let go.

He said we'd seal it together.

He promised.

She reached the edge of the realm, where the ground dissolved into nothingness. There, the wind whispered faintly — a voice she almost recognized.

"Kritika..."

Her breath caught. "Kael?"

The air shimmered, forming a faint outline — his outline. His face flickered in and out, like a reflection on water.

"Kael," she breathed, tears streaming down her cheeks. "Where are you?"

He smiled faintly — that half-smile she hated for how easily it broke her heart.

"I'm where the fire went when it died," he said softly. "In between what was and what will be."

"You said we'd survive this," she whispered.

"I said we'd save it," he corrected. "And we did."

She shook her head, voice trembling. "No. That's not enough. Not without you."

The light around him flickered, fading. "You have to finish what we started. The Heart still beats because of you. Keep it alive."

"Don't you dare fade away from me," she choked.

He stepped closer — though he was more light than form now. "Every time a star falls, it's not dying. It's remembering what it once loved enough to burn for. Don't mourn me, Kritika. Just look up."

And then, he was gone.

The sky above exploded with light. One star — brighter than all the others — cut across the heavens, trailing silver fire behind it.

Kritika fell to her knees, sobbing, her mark glowing faintly in sync with the falling star.

"I remember," she whispered. "I remember everything."

Hours or years later — she didn't know which — the world began to color itself again. Shades of violet, gold, and white spilled across the horizon. The broken constellations realigned, forming new patterns — not the old ones dictated by the Council, but something new. Something born from defiance, love, and loss.

The balance had not been restored. It had been rewritten.

And at its center was her.

Kritika stood tall, her tears drying into resolve. The mark on her wrist pulsed once more — no longer gold or silver, but a soft violet, the color of dusk and rebirth.

She closed her eyes and whispered into the wind, "For every lie I told, I'll now speak a truth."

The realm shimmered. Her voice carried through the stars, awakening worlds she hadn't yet seen.

And far away, beyond the edge of creation, a faint flicker of flame stirred — a reminder that some fires never truly go out.

EPILOGUE – THE STAR THAT STAYED

–•✦•–

The stars looked different now.

Sharper. Quieter. Honest.

Kritika sat on the old rooftop of her childhood home, a mug of cold tea forgotten beside her, and stared at the night sky that had once felt so ordinary. Delhi hummed below — restless, beautiful, alive — unaware that somewhere above, universes had burned and been reborn.

A soft wind brushed her hair. It carried the faint scent of rain and something older — something that smelled like him.

Kael.

Her fingers brushed the mark on her wrist — now faint, violet-gold, a pulse that beat not with power, but memory. She hadn't told anyone what happened. Who would believe her? A girl who once built her life out of lies now held the truth of the cosmos inside her chest.

Sometimes, she still heard him. Not in words — in echoes. The flicker of a candle. The spark before a storm. The low hum of power beneath the world's rhythm.

He was there, in all of it.

Not gone. Just... elsewhere.

The world hadn't collapsed after their sacrifice. It had healed — quietly. She could feel the balance humming beneath every breath of the wind, every heartbeat, every whisper of time. The constellations above had shifted, rearranging themselves into something new — something the old Celestial Council would never have approved.

Two spirals, intertwined — silver and gold. The **Mark of Unity.**

Kritika smiled faintly. "We did it," she whispered.

She had gone back to her life, or at least what was left of it. She taught again, painted again, tried to rebuild the fragments of normalcy. But nothing was truly normal. The world she once knew felt... thinner now, like a veil between realities that she could lift if she wanted.

Sometimes she did.

She'd stand by the window, close her eyes, and see glimpses of the other realms — rivers of light, forests of stars, the temple where the Heart once slept. Each time, her pulse quickened, and she'd whisper into the silence, "I'm still keeping my promise."

And sometimes, the silence whispered back.

One evening, months later, she walked by her old school — St. Helena's — the place where her lies had first started. The gates were still rusted, the banyan tree still stretched across the courtyard like an old memory.

She stood beneath it, looking up through the branches. The night sky framed itself between the leaves — and there, shining brighter than any other, was a single star.

It pulsed once, twice, like a heartbeat.

Kritika smiled through tears. "I know," she whispered. "I see you."

A faint warmth touched her wrist — the mark glowing gently in reply.

She looked up one last time. "When stars fall," she said softly, "they never really leave."

Far above, in the silence between worlds, a faint flicker of flame drifted across the void.

A shadow of a man, cloaked in starlight, looked down at Earth — at her — and smiled.

"Until the skies remember your name again."

The flame burned brighter — then vanished among the stars.

And somewhere, deep in Kritika's heart, the world began to hum again.

Sequel Hook: "When Skies Remembered Her Name"

–•✦•–

The closing line — *"Until the skies remember your name again"* — naturally opens the next installment, where:

- Kritika begins to feel disturbances in the constellations again.
- A **new celestial being** appears, claiming to be sent "in Kael's place."
- The balance she rebuilt starts to crack — not from chaos, but from *love trying to return.*

AUTHOR'S NOTE

–•✦•–

If you've reached this page, thank you for believing in Kritika's journey — and in mine.

When Stars Fell for Her is a story about love that transcends reality, and truth that can shatter even the heavens.

The next chapter of this journey continues in *The Truth They Became*, the final book of *The Starbound Saga*.

Until then, keep your heart open — the stars are still watching.

About the Author

–•✦•–

Deepali is an Indian author and designer who weaves emotion and imagination into stories that blend **reality, spirituality, and fantasy.** Her debut novel *The Lies We Weave* and its sequel *When Stars Fell for Her* explore the fragile beauty of truth, love, and human emotion through a cosmic lens.

She believes stories are how souls remember what they once forgot.

🌐 Visit: www.lotussutrabooks.com

📷 Instagram: @raven.dee.author

✉ Subscribe: *Join the Star-bound Circle for early chapters & cosmic updates.*

ALSO BY DEEPALI

–•✦•–

- *The Lies We Weave* — A psychological drama about the lies that bind us.
- *When Stars Fell for Her* — A celestial romance beyond time.
- *The Truth They Became* — Coming Soon, 2026.

READER CALL-TO-ACTION PAGE

–•✦•–

🖉 Loved the book?

Leave a review on Amazon or Goodreads — your words light up the universe for independent authors!

www.ingramcontent.com/pod-product-compliance
Lightning Source LLC
Chambersburg PA
CBHW062147160726
48282CB00027B/953
9789355922762